Clare's Boutique

Clare's Boutique

Three Stories & One Essay

ERIC GIROUX

ISBN: 978-1-7342240-8-5 (paperback)

Book design by Dan Visel
First printing: 2026

New Salem Books
P.O. Box 600672
Newtonville, MA 02460

newsalembooks@gmail.com

www.newsalembooks.com

For Charlene

Table of Contents

THREE STORIES

Ice Time

IT WAS MID-JANUARY AGAIN, AND TROOP 35 WAS trekking up to New Hampshire to live like beasts for two nights and part of three days in one of our summer camp's vacant lodges, feebly heated by a small woodstove at one end. "Come morning, you'll be pissing icicles," Mr. Gloucester, our scoutmaster, had promised in the Market Basket parking lot, where the carpools gathered. He was always posing as the battle-hardened general. When he thought we had gone to sleep, he would draw the other men into a debate about the best peanut butter. With any luck, I thought, the lake would be frozen over when we got up there. We'd ice fish and play hockey all day Saturday and most of Sunday. Maybe even light a crazy fire on it.

I watched Mr. Gloucester lead the others past the lampposts, no longer costumed in tinsel as Christmas trees, and out of the lot. I was stuck behind in the rump group. I waited nearly an hour alone in the back of Mr. Berry's muggy Buick, its felt upholstery the creepy blood red of Hell's very bowels. At last Jack O'Connor arrived, by foot. Jack O'Connor: best friend in kindergarten, estranged ever since.

"Sorry I'm late," Jack said quietly. He tossed his ratty knapsack between us and belted himself in.

Mr. Berry climbed in front and, adjusting his mirror, said, "Condolences." Jack looked out the window.

Condolences, I thought. For what? I wasn't about to ask. I didn't want to risk becoming friends again with Jack by accident. I had been relieved when, a few years earlier, this troublemaker stayed back in Ms. Coolidge's fourth-grade class. Though Scouts had recently thrown us together, we hardly spoke. I wanted to keep my nose clean. Jack was what my father, an actuary, would have called an "operational risk," a term he used for foolhardy clients.

Mr. Berry shifted to drive and pulled out of the spot. He pumped up the heat and popped in a Pink Floyd cassette with a hippie-dippie lyric about being welcomed to a machine. To suppress that, I put on my Walkman, and Jack played his. I braced myself for a long and awkward ride.

Snowflakes speckled the windshield as we turned onto Route 3 North toward Lowell. By the time we reached the WELCOME-BIENVENUE TO NEW HAMPSHIRE: LIVE FREE OR DIE sign, the storm was pressing down hard. The Buick pushed through, wipers flapping wildly and wheels slipping as it found its grip, then slipping again. I stared into the back of Mr. Berry's sturdy head. He had a Viking's bulk and the red beard to match. It gave an impression of safety and strength.

Truth be told, I didn't know him and had never seen him before. I trusted him, though, and for the same reasons I trusted the other strange men with no familial connection to a Boy Scout who chaperoned those trips: he was a grown-up and they had assigned him to us. I suppose I also assumed some things about Mr. Berry's competence. That he kept his car in working order and knew how to drive it. That he had packed whatever groceries Mr. Gloucester had put on his list, such as the ingredients for bug juice or the just-add-water pancake mix that the patrols used to fry breakfast. That if we blew a tire along the way, he could change it.

That's not exactly right. I wanted to assume these things but couldn't. I was pretty concerned about the last scenario, actually. We'd once been stranded for hours on a dirt road outside Montpelier with a popped tire because my father knew little about cars beyond the mortality tables. The memory of that scary and boring day was crossing my mind like a dust cloud when Jack took off his headphones and nudged me.

"What?" I hit "STOP" on my Walkman.

"We're going the wrong way."

"No we're not."

"I didn't see Wang. And where was Nashua?"

He was right. We didn't pass the Wang Labs towers in Lowell. Nashua usually stuck out too because we knew the tax-free mall. I didn't remember seeing that either.

"Hey," Jack said. He thumped the back of Mr. Berry's bench. "Hey there, fine fellow. We're going the wrong way."

"There's two ways," Mr. Berry said without moving.

"Right way and a wrong way," Jack muttered. He rolled his eyes.

"Seems fair to me," I said. I reminded myself that lots of roads went into New Hampshire. At least two highways. We were on one of those. I prepared to don my headphones again but now Jack had a question.

"You still do that Carrot Club thing?"

"No."

"Too bad," he said, surprising me. "I'd join."

"I asked you to. You said no."

"Did I?"

"Yes."

"Okay, well, that was a mistake."

I remembered the incident. It had happened in early fourth grade, a time when I briefly pitied and idealized Jack. At that age, I tended to do this to any boy who was poor, picked-on, wild, weird, or smelled bad. Jack met all criteria. He peed his pants. When his brother wasn't around to protect him, his mother sometimes locked him out of their trailer and he had to eat dog food. He picked doomed fights with larger boys. He mouthed off to teachers and even to Principal Salemi. I was very close to thinking that anyone like this must have some compensating special goodness, and was probably smart and creative, too. I don't know where I got this notion. Maybe the movies. Whatever the source, my faith in these principles had led me to found the Carrot Club, a home base for recess outcasts. And one day I decided to invite Jack to join us. This was not long after Ms. Coolidge granted him parole from copying *Webster's* and released him back into the milling throngs of afternoon recess. With high hopes, I marched out to the wild grassy field where I always met recruits.

"'Carrot Club,'" he snorted. "Whydja call it *that?*"

"Oh, go suck an egg, Jack."

I turned heel and stomped off.

The answer embarrassed me. You see, I was a carrot addict. I ate them morning, noon, and night. At least three bags per week. A poignant children's movie was behind this. In it, a little girl eats an orange thing that looked to me like a carrot. For a time it empowers her to talk to animals, including a mothering kangaroo, who teaches her about nature. That interested me in carrots and gave my club its name.

Something else may help account for my carrot eating. We were a nervous family. My father had heart troubles, two therapeutic heart attacks before the age of forty. My smart and ambitious mother, a French teacher at the high school, was born scared and often said that she could have done more with her life if she wasn't like that. My sister had once been kidnapped in Kmart and held for ninety minutes before the cops nabbed the culprit over by the water tower and pried her from the trunk with a crowbar. After that, a pall of fear draped us, and my parents kept me away from standard activities like the hockey league and skiing. It was a minor miracle that, out of sheer ignorance, they had let me join Boy Scouts, an organization that practically celebrated fire play. I ate carrots as a kind of fantasy escape from my family's worrying. I was reacting to a life where nature's hazards would never find me alone.

Or so I've been told by a licensed professional. Eventually I had to quit carrots because they had turned me orange. As for the Carrot Club, in fifth grade's twilight I disbanded it. It seemed babyish, like something you couldn't carry into middle school. Also, I no longer believed in unusual boys like Jack who got themselves in trouble.

Mr. Berry's erratic driving had me on edge—it wasn't just slippery roads. I also worried now about our alternate route and wished Jack hadn't brought that up. To distract myself, I fiddled with the cigarette lighter in the door. I looked inside to where it burned orange in three hot rings and was tempted to put my finger there.

"What are you listening to?" Jack asked.

I showed him the Schoolly D cassette case. He showed me his Dead Kennedys: *Bedtime for Democracy.*

"Their last album. They broke up."

I handled my Walkman. "This just came out."

"We should swap."

"Maybe later."

Punk was fading. Rap was on the way up, though in the Lowell suburb where we lived it was not popular. Except, perhaps surprisingly, among the honors kids, the ones most likely to leave town, as I have.

Jack fell silent again.

"What happened?"

"To what?"

"Mr. Berry said, 'Condolences.'"

If he heard his name, Mr. Berry didn't react. He gazed off to the side for what seemed like an abnormal amount of time, like how characters talked while driving on TV.

"Jim died," Jack said. "Left his car in neutral at the IHOP and it rolled over him." His eyes shifted to me. "'Pancaked.'"

"I thought he was in the Army," I stupidly said, as if that should have protected him.

"On leave." He paused. "He wasn't drinking."

"I liked Jim."

"He was sort of like my good dad."

Jim had babysat for me back when Jack and I were kindergarten buddies. Jack came along as a bonus, and Jim conjured a birthday-party atmosphere from Pin the Tail on the Donkey, wrestling, and unruly badminton (we were too young to really play). He was a sporty kid in a headband, full of zest, and I took him for a world-famous athlete. I hadn't seen him since my break from Jack, except for once outside Cumberland Farms. He issued a hearty wave as he drove by with his knockout girlfriend.

"They bury him tomorrow." With his finger he slowly drew on the window a circle face with a straight-line mouth. "In Dracut. I wanted to camp."

I didn't know what to say to that. It seemed like some new kind of badness for Jack to not be there for his brother's funeral.

Despite the shock of this news, I soon became drowsy. My chin drooped, and I fell asleep. Sometime later I jolted awake when I felt the car swerve. It shot off the road into the snow and down a steep bank and, as if aiming, plowed toward a glimmering tree. We smashed into it and my head pounded the front-seat bench. Then it slammed back against the back seat and I bounced forward and my arms flew up. Jack slumped over, groaning. Up front, Mr. Berry seemed fine. His head was back against the headrest like it had always been and his face aimed forward. Pink Floyd still played—we were back to the machine song—and I watched his right arm, expecting it to move up to the shifter to put us into reverse and get us out of this jam. But then I noticed a pinpoint circle in the windshield with lightning-bolt cracks shooting out and Mr. Berry's arm didn't move. Smoke rose from the hood and a small flame flared from a corner.

"Let's get out of here," Jack said, rousing himself. "Thing's gonna blow."

I pulled the lever and rammed my shoulder into the door, but we were on a slant and I was working against gravity. Jack tumbled out his side, then dashed around to mine and wrenched the door open. I climbed out and fell in the snow.

"Get up," he said. "Get up or you'll freeze. You'll get wet and freeze." He lifted me and planted me upright in the snow like a lawn ornament, then lunged for the front door and opened it, stuffed his torso in, and tugged at Mr. Berry. A moment later he grimly emerged. "He's dead."

I stood there dumbly. I couldn't hear that or think or do anything.

"Now put on your hat and gloves." He grabbed me, turned me, and slapped my back to start marching me up to the road. The car didn't blow up, but a streak of heat licked me. At the road he said, "We'll hitch it to a payphone and call for help." He looked up and down the silent black strip.

"I can't."

"I got change, and I bet some restaurant will let us use theirs."

"No: hitchhike," I rasped. After the psycho kidnapped my sister, hitchhiking was about the last thing my parents would have allowed. I couldn't grasp an emergency exception.

"We have to," Jack said. "It's zero out. Maybe less."

While we waited we stomped our feet to keep the blood flowing. Eventually I wondered what time it was and took off my right glove to check my watch but it was missing. I grabbed and patted myself all over. It seemed that if I found my watch I'd be saved, and that if it was lost for good, I probably was, too. Snow encased my hand but I kept searching as my glove tumbled down the bank into the darkness. Stiffness spread across my hand.

"I can't feel it."

"What?" Jack shouted back at me. He was out on the road, cupping his eyes.

"I can't feel my hand."

"Bang it," Jack said.

"What?"

"Bang it on your thigh. Like this." He walked over to me. "Can you feel it?"

"It feels fat like a baseball mitt."

He gripped my shoulders. "Put it in your pants and grab your nuts."

"*What?*"

"Grab your nuts. Like a water bottle."

I stared at him.

"Dang it," Jack said. He took off his own gloves and threw them on the snow, then snatched my bare hand, pulled open my trousers, and shoved my hand down there. The added warmth startled me. I instantly knew it was a good idea. Then Jack turned back to pick up his gloves, only to find that a snowy gale had whisked them away too. "Oh boy. Here we go." He slipped both hands down the front of his pants.

We stood there for a while like that. Snow landed on my cheeks and tunneled into my ear. With my free hand, I yanked down my hat. Look at us grabbing our nuts, I thought. We exchanged a glance. The dam broke, the laughter coming in fearsome waves. "Nuts! Hah hah!" "Hah hah: nuts!" Each time it settled down, one of us would scream "nuts," and we'd explode again.

It only worked for one hand at a time, so Jack tried taking turns, swapping one hand in and one hand out. That didn't work either. Not enough time for either hand. He made some calculation and pulled his left hand up into the arm of his thin jacket—in all my years knowing him, the boy never had the right winter clothes—and grabbed his balls with his right.

"We should talk," he said.

"To keep warm?"

"To stay awake. One of the things that got that guy in 'To Build a Fire' was that his mind went, right?"

"I guess he might've made it if he had someone to talk to."

"Exactly. So say something. Ask me anything."

"Okay. Why aren't you going to Jim's funeral?"

Shoulders hunched, he kicked some snow.

"I don't want to see that. I want to go camping. Jim took me camping a lot. Showed me stuff. Did you know he made Eagle? Whoa, this hand. I can't feel it."

He poked his left fist from the jacket and pounded his thigh with it.

"My turn to ask you something." He gave me a sly look. I thought he was going to mention nuts and prepared to lose it. Instead he surprised me with another funny question: "Am I still cute?"

That went back even further than the Carrot Club! It referred to when we met, the first day of kindergarten. Early September, 1980. A blue sky with fluffy clouds that glowed. We were standing in the long, neat line that led from Boston Road to the doors of the old high school's building, waiting to be marched in. Jack wore an unseasonable brown sweater with holes that recalled my ragged teddy bear Leon, lost at the planetarium. "I think you're cute," I said. He must have taken me in for a moment before saying, "I think you're cute, too." My mother had dressed me patriotically and like my father, in a light sport coat over a red-white-and-blue plaid button-down, khakis, and shiny new loafers. I decided that Jack and I were best friends and announced it.

In first grade—to complete our history—they assigned us to different teachers. In second grade the misbehavior began, and my parents kept us apart. I briefly warmed to him again in fourth grade, as I've mentioned. But leading into middle school he turned into something alien and risible, a bomber-jacket-and-combat-boot-wearing "maggot" who listened to punk. Jim was one, too, along with the rest of that bunch from the park, but I didn't think of him that way. In time they would find their own ugly word for us, the white boys in Pumas who were hooked on rap. The most sacred friendship may founder on such meanness.

Before I could answer Jack's question—he may have regretted it; anything gay-sounding was shameful and forbidden—he was off to a new topic. "The road's closed. I'm not seeing anyone," he said. He looked back down the road once more and then the other way, in the direction we had been going. "Let's hit the trail."

We headed north, snow whipping our faces. I had new Moon Boots that I hadn't broken in, and my shins burned. Jack wore old and too-large tennis sneakers, a surprising departure. Each time he lifted a sneaker from the caking snow he rhythmically shook it like a small bell.

"Let's sing 'On Top of Spaghetti,'" he proposed.

We sang that, and then he started in on "Peanut Butter and Jelly." As we walked, a flashlight stuffed up his sleeve unspooled the next few feet of road.

"Now your pick. Only don't make it about food because now I'm hungry."

I couldn't feel my face but, forcing some cheer, chose another tune. A favorite of mine from a few years back.

"Okay: 'I Love Mud.'"

"I don't know that. You have to start it and then I'll come in. Like a round."

I sang the first verse and then looped it and then Jack joined in after a few bars. Mrs. Smith, our music teacher in elementary school, had taught us that trick. The song was by a Maine folksinger, a regional talent who frequented the family camps. It was about loving mud and, being unable to go around it, guessing he would have to go through it.

"That's just like us," Jack said. "Except snow."

I didn't say anything. Like the others, it was a childish song, more Webelos level than Scouts. But the round gave it a choral flavor that made it sound different. Holy, almost, at least to me. The other reason I'd grown quiet was that during the song my vision had gone hazy. I didn't know if it was the snow hitting my eyeballs or something failing in my brain. And yet, up ahead, I could just make out a blinking orange light.

"You see that?" Jack asked.

"I s-see it," I said, jaw cramping.

"Wait, wait. Time for one more."

We rushed forward while Jack belted out "There's a Skeeter on My Peter (Whack It Off)." I made out three lights, a zigzagging line of sawhorses, and two cop cruisers parked slantways.

"Hey. *Hey.* It's *us!*" Jack shouted, as if we were arriving late for a family reunion. When we reached a cruiser, he waved his arms and his left hand poked out bare and purple. "We made it."

A window slid down a few inches, revealing the top third of

a statie's bald head, eyebrows raised over pointless sunglasses. "Road's closed," a voice croaked. "You can't be here."

Jack rapped the window with his knuckles. "Little pig, little pig, let me in."

Things moved quickly then. They sped us to a clinic and split us up for tests. Later a gurney whisked Jack off to an ambulance that would take him back south to Exter Hospital, where he'd lose his left pinky.

I checked out fine: I could follow a finger and name Vice President Bush. Excited staties gratuitously loaded me onto a snowcat and steered me the last eight miles to the lodge. Mr. Gloucester caught the moment's ceremonial spirit and saluted me at the door. With outstretched palm, he awarded me the bottom bunk nearest the woodstove. After pork and beans we held a small memorial service for Mr. Berry, whose death the shortwave had confirmed. It turned out no one knew him all that well or remembered him signing up for this trip. Was he even supposed to be here? No matter, we were on to dessert: fudge sundaes, compiled from the Igloos (as much as illicit fires, wayward feasting was a Scouts tradition).

There was some loafing time and then Mr. Gloucester sent us to our bunks. The men gathered by the woodstove for late-night yammering, drinking, and cards. Then they, too, went off to bed, and the woodstove's last embers faded. The cold and my full bladder woke me in the wee hours. I slipped outside and took a gratifying piss against a tree. Alone in the whistling woods, I wasn't scared. I wasn't scared at all.

Hamburger Hill

MY FRIEND BILL MIDGE HAD A SISTER NAMED Tammy who was Playmate of the Month in the late 1980s. The spread's theme was horseback riding, which she had a thin connection to from a summer spent at her grandparents' farm in Belchertown. She said on the questionnaire that she hoped to make the world a better place and that *Playboy* would pave the way to Hollywood. When the issue hit the stands, she was an eighteen-year-old senior at the high school and there were lecherous rumblings among the male faculty and staff.

"They all bought it," my mother, who taught French, reported. "Every last one of them."

"Why not? She's legal," my father said.

"She's a kid. *Their* kid. Christ, Mr. Deluca had it splayed out in the faculty room. Why not pin the centerfold to the cork board while you're at it?"

My father winced. "Margaret: the children."

I immediately decided that he, too, had a copy: I'd find it.

"You're both gross. Don't drag me into it," my sister said.

Everyone looked at me. "What? I'm thirteen," I said.

"He knows everything. He listens to rap."

My parents had not yet caught my sister's incessant hints that it was time to inspect the moral sewer that my tape collection had become. She was on to me because I had made the mistake of playing my boombox in the yard and rapping along with gusto to make tolerable the chore of leaf-raking. My current favorite was *Straight Outta Compton*, N.W.A.'s recent debut. Here was a little something about an N-word like me, I unselfconsciously proclaimed. I never should've been released from jail, was insane, smoked plenty of pot, and was recently featured in the newspaper for having killed one or two people, and F-you if you disapproved. In reality I was a suburban white boy who had never *seen* drugs or missed school, let alone committed "a 211" or murder.

Still, there was true feeling in my yard-chore rapping. A week or so earlier, a kid in gym class had scraped up my glasses by dragging them across the locker, and this new rap gave eloquent voice to my middle-school fantasy of vengeance. After all, think of the many horrors Ice Cube and the other members of N.W.A. had inflicted on their urban foes. Drive-bys, gang bangs, cop killings. And yet they walked free. Not only that, but they'd lived on to rap about it. When I listened to a song like "Gangsta Gangsta," I felt that maybe I, too, could go off on a motherfucker, such as the kid who scraped my glasses, with my gat. If only I knew what a gat was and could find one.

After my family's *Playboy* tiff, I went to my room and dialed up Sanjay on my personal phone. My mother had given it to me (not a phone *line*, just a phone) back in sixth grade because of my "expanding social needs." While the phone rang, I hit "PLAY" on my boombox to reanimate Boogie Down Productions' "My Philosophy." This was a running joke. Any time I called Sanjay that tape was playing, as if I needed it to breathe.

He usually answered, and quickly. But this time the phone just rang and rang. I hung up and tried again. He answered on the second ring and laid it on thick with an exaggerated version of his parents' accent.

"Good day, this is Revolting Reddys. May I please take your order? Our special today is curried dicks with a side of fried asshole."

I laughed. "Yo! What if someone else was calling?"

"Fuck 'em," he said, dropping the joke voice.

"Yo, want to play with fire and then come over my house and watch *Yo! MTV Raps* in my basement?"

"Word."

I was referring to the recent premiere. That August, Sanjay had come to stay with us at the Dennis Port rental cottage. When the show aired, we recorded it over my dad's copy of *The Day After*, a terrifying WWIII film from 1983. Then we watched it together a dozen times or more during the otherwise glum week leading into the new school year. *Yo! MTV Raps* was our portal into rap's future. It bridged us from already canonical groups like Run-D.M.C. and the Beastie Boys to the array of acts just then breaking out: EPMD, Too $hort, 2 Live Crew, and more. N.W.A. was too new to be on there. But their stunning debut had miraculously surfaced at the tape store. I found it first and had yet to share it with anyone, including Sanjay.

"Yo, homie."

"Yo."

"*Power* lines."

"Yo!"

We hung up and I went downstairs to grab the gun bag, thinking something was off about Sanjay. The words were normal, but not his voice. It's like it wasn't Sanjay but someone performing Sanjay. I shook this off and dashed back upstairs with the gun bag, then zoomed past my mother to the door.

"I'm going to the woods to play Army." I held up the gun bag.

"Watch out for ticks!"

"Yo, *fuck* them motherfuckers," I growled.

"I *hear* that, mister! Do you want to go out or be grounded till kingdom come?"

I hoisted my boombox and pushed out the door with that dangling from one arm and the gun bag from the other. I had to get my language in check before my parents snuffed out these short bursts of after-school freedom or, just as bad, confiscated "that rap crap" from my tape collection. The gun bag was heavy because it was filled with toy rifles and pistols and, more substantially, my grandfather's machine gun from WWII, which he'd smuggled out of France after shaving off the serial number. Each weapon had served honorably for a few years' worth of Hamburger Hill "reenactments" in the woods between my street and Sanjay's. We didn't know what happened at Hamburger Hill, but our friend Donny's dad, who had nightmares about it, had been there and the name had panache. The gun bag's active ingredients, circa eighth grade, were different: restaurant matchbooks, a pack of firecracker "snakes" and a Roman candle, a cigarette lighter, and a small can of lighter fluid. I'd carefully wrapped these in *The Lowell Sun*'s comics. The guns were just for cover, but the *Sun* served double duty as kindling.

I slung the bag over my shoulder and angled my boombox into my Huffy's front basket, then popped in a classic to serenade me to the "campsite": Run-D.M.C.'s "King of Rock," as performed by Sanjay and me. Sanjay and I had lip-synced it at the seventh-grade dance, stunning everyone with our momentary coolness as we flawlessly snapped back and forth between my Run and his DMC. Later, at Whalom Park, in a "make you a star" studio-booth, we made this tape of ourselves rapping over the music in our thin, elfin voices (I still have it). We were prepared for these challenges because we had rapped together for many hours in my parents' basement. After school, we bounced around down there until the little window steamed up and we collapsed with exhaustion to watch infomercials. Then it got dark and melancholy, and Sanjay had to bike home for supper.

I pedaled around the block to the dirt path that led through the power lines. Some freak was supposed to be out there, an apocryphal and self-contradictory "man who dressed up as a woman and ran around naked" molesting kids. But we'd never caught whiff of him. At the big rock, I turned off the path to our woodsy spot behind our old elementary school and found Sanjay slouching on a log. I unzipped my bag and removed a couple of rifles and the machine gun to reach the fire kit. I tossed Sanjay the paper.

"Yo, twist this."

He tore off a piece and began methodically reshaping it into densely packed kindling.

"Yo, I think I'll make an upside-down cross and set it on fire," I said.

"How could you tell?"

"What?"

"I mean, how could you tell it's an upside-down cross? Are you going to put a Jesus on there and stick him in the ground or something?"

"Maybe."

"Don't you find that a little disrespectful?"

"Yo, what do you care? You're like half a Hindu."

"Yeah, but you're half Catholic."

"Yo! Who's the G with the flaming pentagram, yo? Why you frontin?"

"Yo," he said, meaninglessly, and stared into the woods.

Casting about for a remedy for his black mood, I seized my boombox and swapped out the Run-D.M.C. for N.W.A. I'd been hoarding it so I could master lyrics and become the local expert on this new path for rap. Ordinarily, I'd laboriously wind back to the beginning of the album, or at least the song. But I decided to just play it from where it was, in hopes of jolting Sanjay back to normal. The music began with a chorus of girls singing that they'd like to fuck Eazy-E, and then Eazy replies, with enthusiasm, that he would enjoy fucking them as well.

"What is this shit? Turn it off."

"It's N.W.A.! They're awesome!"

"It's gross the way they talk."

"Yo! What about 2 Live Crew?"

"They're gross, too. I'm sick of this trash."

I hit "STOP" on my boombox.

"Yo, toss me a matchbook," Sanjay said. I noticed he had made quick work of his kindling assignment and threw a couple of the restaurant matchbooks his way. One was from a tiki restaurant, another from an Italian place. My parents, who didn't smoke, collected them in a bowl for commemorative purposes.

Sanjay lit the top of one of his twisted-up pieces of newspaper and held it aloft like a torch. "Hail Satan! By this flame, I command you, Prince of Darkness, to bestow your infernal powers upon us."

"So much for religious piety," I said, busting out a Social Studies term. I considered what he'd said about N.W.A. and 2 Live Crew. "Yo, are you gay? Because if you are, I really need to know that."

I swore to myself that if the answer was yes, I'd be okay with it. I'd say congratulations or something, like he'd won a special prize. Of course that'd be trailed by my revulsion at the imagined ickiness of gay sex and my fear of AIDS. I knew you couldn't transmit AIDS by sweat, just by blood or semen. But a *lot* of sweat? A *lot* of breathing the same air? I thought back to our abundant basement time, and, a few years before that, my mother's warning in Provincetown, that I shouldn't eat a hot dog there because a resentful AIDS patient/hot-dog maker might've spat in it.

"I think my dad might be. I think my dad's a faggot."

"Your dad's not a fag. Why would you say that?"

"What do you care about my dad? You make fun of him."

"You make fun of him."

"That's different."

"Okay, sure. But he can't be gay. He has a wife. He has a kid. *You're* his kid. What more proof do you need?"

"That just means he—what—screwed one time? I screwed a glove. Does that make me not gay?"

"Are you?"

"I don't think so. Are you?"

"Fuck no."

I was so shaken that I barely noticed he'd admitted jerking off. This was not something we acknowledged at thirteen, even though Health class had taught us that it, like being gay, was normal. Healthy, even. "You all do it," gross Coach Zawatsky said. "In fact, you should." I know I did, but I was deeply ambivalent about my practice.

"Why do you say your dad's a … gay man."

"I just know."

He tossed his newspaper torch in the burn pit.

"How do you know?"

"If I tell you, you have to swear never to tell anyone. Because if you do, I'm dead. I'm fucking dead. And if I'm not dead? I'll kill myself."

"Yo: yes."

"They arrested him last night."

"He's in jail?"

"He's back home now. It's not like a big crime. Though it's bad enough."

"What did he do?"

"Yo, toss me that Roman candle."

He stepped away from the campsite to light it, then held it

to his groin and spewed its contents at random into the woods. I tried to follow the stars to their landing places, idly wondering if any would take hold and start a small fire for us to play with.

"You know the rest area on the highway?" he said, still facing the woods. "The one we stopped at once when we went roller skating? We got hamburgers there or something. Heh, my dad paid for them. We ate the burgers on this hill out back where there was an extra parking lot, like out under the trees. It's where everyone went to park and eat their burgers. Even half Hindus."

"Those were good burgers. Your dad got us seconds, right? Milk shakes, too."

I also remembered that car ride as the first time I saw elephant-headed Ganesha (the god of new beginnings, I've learned since), mounted on Mr. Reddy's dashboard.

"Well, they caught him and like ten other guys out there at two a.m."

"Eating *burgers*?"

He turned and looked at me. "They were screwing, Clarence." He lit two more newspaper torches and carried them over to a small pile of leaves next to a tree and dumped them. "Fucking Hamburger fucking Hill."

I didn't know what to say. There were some rough scripts then for talking to a friend who told you he was gay. Coach Zawatski had a whole worksheet on it. But there was no instruction for this. So I was glad in a way that Sanjay launched a fresh and more urgent crisis by lighting one match after another and tossing them hither and thither.

"What the fuck are you doing?"

"We've talked about this."

"Not *now*."

The leaf pile by the tree had flared up. Over Sanjay's shoulder,

I saw another fire going, from a Roman candle shell.

"It's the perfect time. I want to light it."

"Did you even check?"

"I came that way and didn't see anyone. You came the other way and didn't either, right? It's a victimless crime. Except maybe some squirrel."

While he spoke the flames rose in little piles around him.

"Jesus, it's fucking hot," I said.

"It's fire, asshole."

He was right that we had talked about this before, moving on from campfires and satanic flaming circles and pentagrams to a true-blue forest fire. The closest we'd gotten was when I got carried away with lighter fluid, and then it was the typically poised Sanjay who had pushed me aside into the cool shadows and thrown his coat over the fire to smother it.

"Come on, man, let's put it out."

I rushed around stomping out small fires with my shoes. But there were so many of them that it was like tap dancing. Through the smoke, I saw Sanjay pull a little smile.

"No."

"Well, fuck you, then. I'm out of here!"

I loaded my boombox back onto my Huffy, left the gun bag to burn, and lifted my foot to the pedal.

"Run, you idiot! Who *cares* about your dad."

He stared at me, a wall of flames behind him, then turned and walked away.

Was *I* gay and didn't know it? I wondered as I biked home. What about all those hours Sanjay and I had rapped and wrestled. That seemed pretty gay. Then again, I'd never gotten a hard-on. But maybe that would change now, with his father's sordid tale contaminating my mind?

I thought of a simple way to sort this out: *Playboy*, the one with Bill's sister. The specially charged hotness of a known girl naked could quickly prove that I hadn't turned gay—or that I had. If I didn't get hard, I figured I was done for. I may as well bike out to Hamburger Hill and get on with my new lifestyle.

I found it right away, two mags deep in my father's closet stash. I stuffed it under my T-shirt and hurried to my room, where I tore it open and ripped past all the news and fiction crap—to Tammy Midge's glorious spread. For one picture, she'd mounted a horse. In another she lounged on her bed's rolling silk, exposing her brown "vagina" (the Health-class term, not one of the more colorful synonyms from rap, sprang to mind). Her whole stance was majestic: commanding and inviting, proudly nude. Every look said, "Yes, I want you, but I have many options." To my enormous relief, I passed with flying colors. Then I leisurely read through Tammy's questionnaire and returned the issue to its hiding place.

Sometime after supper, my mother hollered that Sanjay was on the phone. I was in my room, completing a mindless binder-organizing exercise for my study-skills class while playing N.W.A.'s "Fuck Tha Police" on my boombox. I decided to leave the music on but turned it down a notch before answering.

"Yo, Ma, I got it! Hang up!" I waited for the click. "Yo."

"Yo: he didn't do it. It was just some mix-up. He was there, but it didn't go down like that at all. He went in for a shake and got caught in the dragnet. Those asshole staties won't believe him, but they don't know my dad."

I considered this for a moment and said, "Yo: *fuck* tha po-lice!" I held the phone up to my boombox. It was at the chorus, where they loop Eazy-E declaiming the song's title over record scratches.

"Yo, that's def," Sanjay admitted. "You know I'm not gay either, right?"

"Yo."

"Are you? Because it's cool if you are, yo."

"No, yo."

"Yo! See you in school."

I hung up and threw on my Scout uniform for my troop meeting at the elementary school. My mother gasped as we entered the parking lot. Three fire engines were pulling out of the woods behind the baseball diamond.

Yo, I thought. We did it.

Stickup

I DIDN'T ALWAYS MAKE MOVIES. FOR A FEW months after college I ran a small store in the Lowell, Massachusetts, suburb where I'd grown up. The store sat on a shuttered parcel I had inherited from my father, who had once owned a store there and had died that spring, as long expected. What did Slipt Disc offer the discerning consumer of the late 1990s? Appropriately, dead and dying things: used records, tapes, and CDs, with a specialty in rap, the music of my childhood. There was also some blues and folk that I had whimsically included in my bulk order from a similar joint in Haverhill that was failing. I played it a lot on the store Hi-Fi. I liked Bo Carter's raunch and Jean Ritchie's chaste soprano and how Lead Belly sang that when he woke up in the morning, blues was all in his bread (got it). Fresh to me, the old music seemed to carry me along like a bindle to the future.

That future, as I saw it, was "the law." I'd been admitted to a Midwestern law school with a partial, need-based grant and planned to start, on a delayed basis, in the spring semester. I'd found it oddly gratifying at my father's wake when Mr. Hitch, a libertarian social-studies teacher with whom I'd once butted heads like rhinos over gun control, congratulated me on my practical career choice.

"Good for you, Clare. Wish I'd done that. I know your dad would be proud."

He was, but Mrs. Greene, my favorite English teacher, showed up at the wake with a different opinion.

"Do you *want* to be a lawyer?"

"I'm not sure."

"Don't go to law school if you don't want to be a lawyer."

She bear hugged me and, in addition to apologizing for my father's death, muttered in my ear: "You've changed."

A teacher's curse if ever there was one—I wanted to bolt like Fredo! She must have been so disappointed. She'd favored me as a student writer. I reminded her, she once confided, of her hero, Lowell-boy Jack Kerouac, and, by extension, of her own freewheeling days in 1950s Hoboken. Jack Kerouacs don't go to law school.

I was speechless but could hear my father's ghost rise up in my defense. *She just wants nobody to grow up like she didn't.* It was a view he held of most teachers, and I'm not sure my mother was an exception. If I was becoming a practical man—if I was going to dodge the shoals of the whole "Live Your Dream" ethos painted across the high-school theater department's long concrete wall—I owed it to my father and these kinds of hard-nosed sentiments. I knew that. I was grateful for it. But then why the recurring nightmares?

I had another one after the wake. I was standing (naked, of course) at a chalkboard at the front of a crowded law-school lecture hall. Mrs. Greene rose from her seat near the back. She pointed at me with her claw and released a screech that sounded exactly like—spoiler alert—zombified Donald Sutherland in *Invasion of the Body Snatchers* (1978). The next morning I stared in the mirror and tried to imagine myself, grayed and wrinkled, as a law-firm partner at the advanced age of fifty. Had it all been worth it, this life of hours (est. total: 55,000, spread out over twenty-six years) billed for commerce?

As you may have gathered, the store wasn't a big part of my plans. It was just a holding place while my mother and I mourned. (No wallower, my sister had driven straight from the lawyer's office to her flight back to Madison and her grad-student hovel.)

My nominal goal was to build up the store and sell it for a small profit before I started law school. If I was lucky, I would gin up enough cash to keep me in pizzas and escapist trips to the movies for a year. In the meantime, I would survey my customers for girl-friends. Or at least a date, if only to distract me.

One day, in an unpleasant break from the store's monotony, Uncle Mike, who had skipped my father's funeral, dropped by with flowers.

"Rich yet?"

"*You* made a killing."

"We *lost* a killing. Repeatedly." He smiled his everyone's-al-ways-screwing-me smile as he slid the vase onto the counter. "Peo-ple won't come here for anything."

"I would've paid anything for your stickers."

"You didn't have anything."

"Still don't."

"And soon you'll have less."

He looked about my woefully barren store like he was sizing up a dog turd to fling at me.

"Remember when we used to have candy and toys all up and down here? All the way up: up, up to the ceiling. All sorts of goodies."

"Baseball cards, too," I said, to jolt him.

It was a sore point, the reason my father had fired him. Be-fore that break—a more definitive rupture than it seemed at the time—the store had been Uncle Mike's, or seemed to be because he ran it day-to-day. My father was buried in his real work, as an actuary for the auto-insurance company. He didn't much like it but felt it was normal, as in *typical* or *to be expected*, to dislike your job. Meanwhile, Uncle Mike, who palpably did like his job, paced the aisles like a panther, aggressively hawking a fantastic assortment of comics, stickers, cards, hobby kits, magic tricks, tin robots, college banners, sports paraphernalia, earth clay, penny candy ("Chinese" gum), gags—you name it. To us kids, it was Uncle Mike's stuff. Why didn't he take it all home for himself? Or live here? (Depending on your age, you may need to extrapolate from Minecraft to grasp my nostalgia. This type of shop, with its avalanche of boyish kids' stuff, is gone now—vanished, except maybe in Vermont.)

To my surprise, none of this splendor made money. And after a while, Uncle Mike had brought on his crafty "associate" Lenny, who cooked up a good cop, bad cop scheme to screw little kids out of their baseball-card wealth with dirty trades. A boy came in with a Yaz, and Lenny laid right into him.

"I don't know what daddy said but that's a second-year card. Practically worthless."

"Best Sox player ever," Uncle Mike interjected.

"What about Ted Williams?" the kid asked.

"Or Cy Young," Lenny said.

"The Babe," the kid said.

"I'm an idiot," Uncle Mike said. "Forget I breathe."

Eventually they beat the kid's Yaz down so far he was willing to trade for a Steve Lyons rookie, which really was worthless.

"Screwed myself again," Lenny said, while the kid was in earshot.

"You can't help it. No one can. Why do I try?"

I'd watched this play out a few times. Lyons for Yaz. Yaz for Mantle. Mantle for a '62 Maris. The heady climax came with a failed Ty Cobb "Bat Off Shoulder" deal. The grandfather had the wits to step in (after all, it was his card), and he reported it to my father via Mr. Odell, our neighbor, at a V.F.W. spaghetti dinner. That night my father cornered me in the kitchen and pumped me for details. The next day he fired both men, said he wanted them out of the store, pronto. Uncle Mike mounted a belated defense from behind the counter.

"You're so self-righteous. Your whole business is arbitrage. And now you're mad because me and Lenny do it better?"

"I can't have this stink. Mikey, you're done."

Now I knew whose store it really was: my father's and, at one remove, mine. This brought me little immediate joy, though, because that night at dinner my father was still fuming.

"This is how he thanks me!" he shouted, and then blurted out a family secret that he'd held in for years but would now speak of freely till the day he died, so that Uncle Mike and all around him would think about it when they heard his name. "Clarence Renault: What do we think of a deli clerk who swipes hams from his elderly boss's beleaguered grocery store and then trades them out of a pickup truck for drugs? Is that a good man? Is that someone we'd like to emulate?"

"No, sir."

"I *gave* him that job and he screwed me!" His eyes blazed at me.

"*Clare* didn't do it," my mother pleaded.

"Yeah, Dad. Lay off," my sister said. "And language: please," she added, before looking me dead in the eye and gratuitously calling me a shithead again.

To replace Uncle Mike and Lenny, my father hired a recent high-school grad whose probity had impressed him at a Rotarian of the Month luncheon. He let me help that dope after school, my sweet reward for ratting.

Incidentally, my father would not have liked that I'd returned to open a store on the old site and scout girls there. Illness and work had stranded him, he said, in this defunct hog town and he'd move back to his classier, seaside hometown of Hingham in a flash if he could. That his antipathy extended to local girls became clear one night during high school, when my girlfriend Dana dumped me in a baffling way and I returned home in tears to tell all. (I was abnormally obliging and confiding for a teenager.)

"She doesn't want to see me again. Not only that. She said she never was my girlfriend. Which is nuts. We made bracelets to prove it. Look."

I rolled up my rugby shirt's sleeve.

"It's a fine bracelet, son." He pinched my sleeve, rubbing the fabric between his fingers. "Nice shirt. Cotton?"

I wore that ugly shirt, khakis, and boat shoes to look like a preppy, my idea of how a boy impressed his date as on-the-way-up. This worked except when it spectacularly didn't. I'd also seen a youthful picture of my father dressed like this, back in his Hing-ham salad days.

"I didn't know you could even do that. Nullify a relationship. Like, at that low a level."

He scrunched up his face, preparing, I feared, another lecture on the actuary's tools. So helpful, he claimed, for assessing risk in every situation, not just gruesome death and maiming. After those lectures, it was like he had darkened a few more of the many light-framed doors that opened to my future. And yet his firm warnings brought a kind of relief that settled in later, the relief of decision. The same feeling rushed over me again years later when I dropped my Hollywood dreams and set my bow for law school.

When my father finally opened his mouth, it wasn't an actu-arial lecture that came out but something else constricting and familiar (and to the Bay Staters of today about as musty as hose-and-breeches): a Kennedy-family parable.

"Old Joe told the boys don't run in Massachusetts. You'll get tied down in petty local issues and Beacon Hill corruption. Even if you reached the Corner Office, they'd sink you. No, he told Jack and Bobby, start national and run for Congress. Stay above the fray."

He gave me "a meaningful look." I stood up shaking and pointing.

"Kennedy's a *snob*! *You're* a snob! Dana's *great*—and *I love her!*"

My Hollywood dreams, I should explain, had not been trivial. I already had them back then, in high school. Spike Lee's glorious early run from *Do the Right Thing* through *Malcom X* got me started. Then I signed up for the high-school musical, and in college I directed a stage play. The summer after junior year, I wrote a semi-autobiographical screenplay called *Ghettoblaster*. It concerned a nerdy white boy roaming Cape Cod blasting rap and his parents' Beach Boys while having some preliminary success with a girl he met at the beach. (The girl was wholly fictitious.) I rode the creative high through the grueling manual process of formatting and binding it, then entered it in some costly and hopeless contests. Later, it embarrassed and disgusted me, all that vulgarity and naked self-disclosure. But I'd enjoyed writing it and knew I could do better. (Still like the title.)

The old bells jangled and a girl walked in—a ghost, of sorts, of the very night I just mentioned. Uncle Mike raised an eyebrow.

"Come on," I said.

She was too young. Late high school, was my guess. Uncle Mike gave a take-what-you-can-get shrug and returned to flipping through CDs. He knew I was looking for a girl and supported it. It added zest and intrigue to his life.

"Is that your car outside?" the girl asked. She took off her sunglasses.

"I don't have a car."

"You're blocking me in."

"I'll move it," Uncle Mike said. He squeezed my shoulder and slid past me to the door.

The girl looked confused. "Aren't you going too?"

"Why would I go?"

"Aren't you, like, his nephew?"

"We aren't making sense," I said. But something else was coming into focus. "You look like Dana Burns. Are you little Katy?"

"In the flesh."

This wasn't entirely happy news. Even years later, the breakup with Dana left a taste. I still had our bracelet in my old room, somewhere in my desk.

"Can I get you something?"

She looked at her sandaled toes.

"How old are you? I mean, what grade are you in now?"

"Fourteen, if there was one. Only I'm not in school. I'm broke."

There was something dusty and browned about her, like she'd camped all day and night on a beach. She looked like a smaller and damaged version of her sister, but no less attractive for that. I recalled the May weekend when I had kissed Dana for the first time, in their driveway while my "Creep" single played. That was Saturday night. On Sunday morning, I rose early and hiked from our house up the steep hill for a newspaper as spring charged forward all around me, leaves blooming full and verdant beneath a bright-blue sky and neon pollen dusting the streets. I thought (nerdly), "With this kiss under my belt, I'm not a boy anymore. I'm a young man!" And now, standing in my dusty store across from Dana's kid sister, I suddenly felt like an old one.

"Actually,"—she looked up, round blue doe-eyes framed by black hair crossing smudged cheeks—"actually, I came here to rob you."

"Will you?"

"I don't think so. I thought that was your car."

I pieced it together. She would trick me into leaving the store unattended, then raid the register—or fail to (it was locked). It was such a poor plan that I wanted to rescue her from it. I thought of another blues lyric. If it wasn't for bad luck, she wouldn't have no luck at all.

"We don't have much," I said. Our stock, like the Steve Lyons rookie, was proving damn near worthless. The best stuff, the blues and folk, didn't sell at all. It made no sense. I had begun to suspect I wasn't cut out for business.

The bells jangled again and Uncle Mike was back. He squinted and wagged his finger at Katy.

"I *know* you. What are you doing here really?"

I opened the register and removed its sole contents, a twenty I had slipped in there at the beginning of the week for good luck.

"Donations," I said. "For the food pantry."

"A shakedown."

"It's not a shakedown."

Katy plucked the twenty from my fingers. "It's a stickup."

Uncle Mike paused to take this in. "You're both crazy. I'm going to lunch."

This meant Charlie's Wings. Moments later, Uncle Mike reappeared on a stool over there and was biting into a fat drumstick while staring out the window back across the street at us.

"Some people don't care how silly they look, as long as they can snoop," Katy said.

I hoped she might linger and talk now, but after briefly picking through my counter rack of tapes, she left. Okay, I thought, I'll call her. It was her sister's number and carved in my brain (I could dial it even now). I counted back—one, two, three years—to calculate her age: nineteen or twenty to my twenty-two. Not so creepy.

"Crack whore," Uncle Mike said when he got back.

"What do you know? That's right: nothing."

"She's been a pest for years. Got hooked up with this fried-dough seller in Lowell. Round guy with a big black beard like Bluto. Had a truck and everything. Did a nice business at games and fairs but a whole lot better with this sideline. And Miss Katy here, the things she's done." He looked out the window. "Still pretty though."

I followed my uncle's gaze to the town center, where Katy had crossed the traffic and was examining, with apparent care, the cast-bronze Union solider.

"Very," I said.

That night my mother made our favorite, chicken parmesan. She ate slowly, and I didn't rush to leave her. I think I was the only person she'd seen all day at the house, except maybe Dayle the mailman in his one-doored blue Jeep. I considered asking her about Katy, but I'd heard enough for one day from Uncle Mike. Why did I need to pry into her troubles, if I wasn't going to help her?

"Hand me those bills," my mother said.

I nudged the Lazy Susan so the bills and her checkbook and pen were in front of her. She set her half-eaten pasta aside, removed this bit of work, and started in on it.

"You'll be pushing off soon, then," she said while signing a check.

"Not yet, Ma. It's June. We have months."

"Forgot that part. You're starting late." She sealed the envelope with a lick. "Phone," she said, then opened the next one. "Electric."

A bill or two later, she repeated, apropos of nothing, something that she'd said to me at least twice already, in slightly different ways, since the funeral. "Your father would be happy with your plans."

As far as I knew, she was too. But then she was cut from an older cloth. It was rare that she'd second guess my father in our presence.

I covered her hand. "What's wrong?"

"I'm not sick."

"Good." I scooped up the bills. My humble contribution was dropping them in our mailbox and raising the flag. "In a few years, I'll be able to help you."

"Won't need it. You and your father had it built up that I'm desperate. I have seven more years, and then it's my pension and off to St. Pete. All my girlfriends will be there. I even insured a grave. Bought it on a *lark* when I was a *spring chicken.*"

She smiled at this. Her habitual punning had confused and frustrated my father to no end.

I didn't call Katy but thought about her so much that a week or so later she stopped by again. This time *she* brought flowers. I added them to the spooky stash growing on my counter. No store, not even a florist's, should recall a mortuary.

"Where's my twenty?"

"What twenty?"

She wandered the aisles, then returned to the counter and said, "Hey, guy, remember that time you saved me?"

"I wouldn't call it that."

"You did. I was drowning, and you pulled me out."

"It was just a crummy pool. Anyone could have done it. Anyone *would* have done it, if I didn't."

"I couldn't swim and no one else was paying attention. No doubt about it. You saved me."

Maybe, but it had caused me trouble back home. "You could've slipped on that wet plastic and snapped your spine in a heartbeat," my father said. "You know you only have one, right? There isn't an extra." "I was careful enough," I said, part of me thinking, "You can't think like that and do much," while the rest of me agreed I'd been stupid.

"What kind of music do you like?" I asked her, to change the subject.

"Different stuff. Cibo Matto, Daniel Johnston. Have you heard Elliott Smith? I still like old-school rap."

"Define 'old school.'"

"Beastie Boys. Run-D.M.C."

"That's not old school. Doug E. Fresh is old school. Slick Rick is old school."

"Ricky D is old school. Slick Rick is new school."

"You're right," I admitted, impressed by her distinction. Slick Rick was Ricky D, just a new name. But a larger change had happened right around then. "I miss those days when rap was like a fun sport with colorful personas."

"Like pro wrestling?"

"Yeah, but I liked the more serious stuff, too. Like 'Fight the Power.' Or the reflective ones on everyday topics. Do you know 'Friends' by Whodini?"

"Don't become lovers until you are friends!" she paraphrased, impressing me again.

Some context for this banter may help. We didn't have a lot of older rap fans in our town, which was nearly all white. Especially rare were older *girl* rap fans. It was only blind luck, in the shape of loving neighbors, that brought the music to me. The Odells, one of the town's few Black families, lived across the street and joined us each Christmas Eve for cocktail wieners and Swedish meatballs, the exchange of gifts, and my mother's rare electric-organ performance. The Odell twins, who were ten years older than me, knew about rap because they'd kept up their connections to East Cambridge, where they used to live. As rap blossomed in the mid-to-late eighties, they gave me a long train of inspiring cassettes, from Whodini's *Escape* (1984) through De La Soul's *3 Feet High and Rising* (1989). I played them all the time. I even played my rap tapes while doing outdoor chores (though I had the good sense not to blast the more profane entries, such as N.W.A. or 2 Live Crew—my own additions to the collection—while painting the Odells' porch). I introduced the music to my friends with great success, and even to Dana, who hated it. The impact went beyond my taste in music. More consequentially, the Odells' gifts led me indirectly to Spike Lee, and to a deeper love for film.

"You don't hear stuff like that anymore."

"It is good. But you're an old deaf man."

"*Def?*"

"*Deaf:* D. E. A. F."

"Maybe a little."

"Find new music."

"I did."

I put on "Death Letter," the Son House song about getting an early-morning letter that his wife had died. He visits the morgue and sees her on the cooling board. Then he goes home miserable. *Finis.*

"New to me," she allowed, adding, "I like that sad song."

I played another, Blind Lemon Jefferson's "See That My Grave Is Kept Clean," about a man running out of time, and let it hang over us like a curse.

"Oooh, this gives me chills."

"Me too."

"It happened another time at Point Sebago," she said, when the song was over.

That was the camp that the teacher families went to. My mother taught high-school French. Dana and Katy's mother managed the special-needs room in the town-hall basement.

"I don't know what you're talking about," I said, though I had an idea.

"I was on a boat. A kayak. A storm blew up and I floated away. And you were there, with my moronic sister who ignored me. But you saw and rushed out to snag my rope."

"They had lifeguards. I'm sure you would've been fine. It was just a little wind."

"Not by my lights. There was an evil black cloud all across the lake."

"How can a cloud be evil?" I asked, though I knew how things can flash intent. In my father's last months his medical equipment ensnared him. It was there to buffer him on a thin cushion of life, but it looked like a strangulation. Even the life-saving function seemed tainted by malice. It was as though it wanted to extend his pain. To stretch it out, like the long emerald tubing that connected him to the oxygen pump and chased him through the house.

"It can. It was," she said, defending her cloud. "You saved me from that storm and from drowning."

She picked up my *Introduction to Contracts* hornbook, which, with another touch of poor salesmanship, I left open on the counter, and flipped through it.

"Why would you read this?"

"I'm going to law school."

"Jeepers creepers: this is *dry*. Can you actually really truly *like* this?"

"I don't know."

She eyed me skeptically. "I don't know either, bub."

"It'll be nice to have something to fall back on."

"But you're not 'falling back.' This is Plan A you're talking."

She set her hand down on the counter like she was chopping it, her fingers pointing directly at me.

"Look here," she said. "I go straight forward like this, and ten years later, I go through you to that wall. But I turn like that"—she shifted her hand to the left by just a few degrees—"and I'm way over there at that Wu-Tang poster. Shift right"—she moved her hand again—"and I'm over there sucking a wing at Charlie's next to your mean old uncle who needs to wipe his face again."

I looked up across the road. Sure enough, Uncle Mike was back over there. Was he following me? Was she? Were they *coordinating*? All these judging eyeballs. Why did they seem to care more about my future than I did? I'd been out of a small town for too long and had forgotten.

"A small change now makes a big difference later," I said, reducing her statement to its moral.

"Bingo and don't I know it." She pitched a thumb over her shoulder. "And if you aim the wrong way, you can't just hit reverse to fix it. Not without one big hairy mess. And hate to break it, pal, but I don't see lawyer here. I see artsy-fartsy type. Which reminds me: you were great in *Brigadoon*."

"So you were stalking me in high school, too!"

"Maybe," she said, grinning.

I had a sudden, forehead-smacking realization. I knew who had made her a rap fan: me.

We talked music some more after that (we both liked Beck and wondered where he'd go next) but I believe she had said her piece because soon she begged off, saying, "Tonight's karate. I'm snatching a nap." Uncle Mike watched her leave and marched right over with his commentary.

"You can save someone but maybe only once," he said, a balanced-sounding yet obscure line that my father might have given and would certainly endorse. I think Uncle Mike said this for my father, because he couldn't be there to shield me with his caution. I knew where that caution had come from: parental fear and love. But it also came from a quiet pain that was personal to my father and that I did not have to inherit or share, even if he had wanted me to (he didn't).

With this gesture, perhaps penitential, Uncle Mike headed for the door. When he opened it, the bells snapped off and one broke loose and rolled into the street. Uncle Mike watched it go.

"I do believe this store is jinxed," he said.

He may have been right. My little shop folded at summer's end. In September, I told my mother I'd be gone all day at the UMass Lowell library. "To study," I said vaguely, but I'd tossed the law books and was plotting my move out West.

ONE ESSAY

Novels as Albums (And Albums that Influenced My Novels)

Novels are Sort of Like Albums

I wish I had picked the guitar as my instrument rather than the saxophone. Once you age out of high-school band, there aren't a lot of good ways or places to play the saxophone, unless you are serious enough to learn jazz improvisation, which I wasn't. Worse still, if you love words and performing them for people (I'll cop to that), the first thing you do as a saxophone player is plug your mouth with the horn. No more words!

But I didn't learn guitar. Or songwriting. And I'm almost fifty. So I'll never be a music star, and I'll never cut an album. That's too bad. There is still a big audience for music, a much smaller one for novels. There's also an appealing immediacy and directness to the best songs and an energizing, visceral connection when personally performing—you get a shadow of it doing karaoke—that is just not there for novelists. You don't have to hit it big to garner some of these rewards, either. You just need a band and an open mic at a bar that has people in it.

But in a removed sense I have had a life in music. All writers do. Poetry descended from song, and words, whether in poetry or prose, can have all the sonic effects they teach you in English classes: assonance, consonance, alliteration, etc. There are also the bad sounds to be avoided, such as unintentional rhymes in prose.

Modernists folded these and other effects from poetry into some of the best prose ever written in English. They also imported poetic repetitions and reversals to produce a range of effects, from galloping to lulling. Take the opening paragraph of James Joyce's "Two Gallants" (repeated words and sounds emphasized by me, and I'm surely missing some):

> The *grey warm evening* of August had de*scen*ded upon the *city* and a mild *warm air*, a *memory* of *summer*, circulated in the *streets*. The *streets*, *sh*uttered for the re*pose* of *Sunday*, *swarmed* with a gaily colored crowd. *Like illumined* pearls the *lamps shone* from the *summits* of their ta*ll* poles upon the *living* texture be*low* which, *changing shape* and hue *unceasingly*, sent up into the *warm grey evening air* an *unchanging unceasing* murmur.

I read some critic describe the effect there as hypnotic. Same goes for the last lines of "The Dead," which evoke the sensation of staring at falling snow (though notice that—again as in music—he *hears* the snow):

> His *soul swooned slowly* as he heard the *snow falling faintly* through the universe and *faintly falling*, like the *descent* of their *last end*, upon a*ll* the *living* and the *dead*.

At least since sometime in the mid-1960s, there's also been a connection between rock and pop albums and novels. At that time, artists like Bob Dylan, the Beatles, and the Beach Boys began conceiving of albums as whole projects with some level of thematic, stylistic, or conceptual overlap or integration. There was ambition for a bigger, fuller statement, where the songs built on one another, rather than just consisting of a few disconnected hits and some B-sides. The order of songs, or the transitions between them, became crucial on something like *Pet Sounds*, conceived as a "teenage symphony to God," as Brian Wilson put it, or on *Sgt. Pepper's Lonely Hearts Club Band* (though Lennon apparently refused to let McCartney's band-within-band concept suffuse the whole project). The ambition went beyond even producing an album full of tracks that each individually warranted a close listen. They were to go together, in whatever loose way and for whatever reason. (Jazz musicians like Miles Davis blazed the album-as-album path sooner, but without words.)

For me, the process of writing and revising a novel seems a bit like what I imagine putting an album together in a studio would be like, and thinking of it that way has made it more fun to write books.

The album-making-like aspects of the process that come to mind include:

- structuring the book, plot-wise;
- deciding where I can trim (thereby accelerating the reading experience) or where I can extend the text and either slow down or—if it's later in the book—ride the narrative momentum so that extension does not result in a slowing down;
- combining those things to think about how long or short each chapter should be in relation to those around it and to the novel as a whole, so that I achieve the desired rhythm and pacing;
- pacing the mood or tonal shifts, so that, for example, there isn't an excess of wacky humor in one place and I'm not overstaying my welcome anywhere if I can help it (I think I did this better in my leaner second novel, *Zodiac Pets*);

€ using the sonic effects noted above in ways that sound good in the reader's ear; and

€ aiming for an overall experience of fullness or satiation for the reader, with the hope that some readers may even find a repeat "listen" appealing.

Of course, the extent to which I achieved any of this is for readers to decide.

Some specific albums, through their sensibility, technique, and linguistic playfulness, have influenced my novels too. I'll tip my hat here to a few by Beck and one by Bob Dylan that I've learned much from—in part, no doubt, because of the impressionable time in my life when I encountered them.

ODELAY *through* MIDNITE VULTURES

The first of the Beck trilogy was *Odelay* (1996), which I had on cassette and took with me to Orlando, Florida, in 1997–98, the year after college, when I had deferred law school to try to become a novelist while playing an undead bellhop at Walt Disney's "*The Twilight Zone* Tower of Terror" (Leo, Stevie Wonder, and NSYNC came through my line).

I had three other albums on constant rotation that year, each of which loomed large in my imaginative and emotional life:

€ *Nashville Skyline*, which made me think of my ex-girlfriend up in New York ("the girl from the North Country"), who might still have been my girlfriend at that time. I couldn't tell. Her position seemed to shift from phone call to phone call.

€ *OK Computer*, which, together with *Crime and Punishment*, Bernard Malamud's *The Assistant*, and *The Letters of Vincent van*

Gogh, made me think about how sad and lonely I was, lower than I'd ever been. It wasn't just the girl trouble or impending law school. Bad nutrition played a role. I wasn't eating well, or enough. Mostly black coffee and two daily packs of Lipton Rice and Sauce Mix: Cheddar and Broccoli ("under new management," it's still on the market). I was basically starving myself while mega-dosing on sodium. I caught six colds that year. I somberly paced the apartment, which I shared with my brother (who footed the $600 rent), in a gray hoodie that my bony frame needed. My brother kept the joint ice cold, a welcome relief to him after a day at the sweltering and circus-like Walker Middle School, where he miserably taught eighth-grade math that year, but I found the powerful AC-blower oppressive.

☾ Philip Glass's soundtrack to *Kundun*, a film that made me think I was a serious, wise, peaceful, and potentially very holy person. Much like the Dalai Lama. I saw the movie maybe five times that year at Disney's megaplex, treating each sitting as a quasi-religious experience, and I could be heard to recite the last lines around the apartment, much to my brother's consternation: asked if he's the Lord Buddha, the Dalai Lama replies that he's like the moon's reflection on water, and that other men, seeing him trying to be good, see themselves. (Right. Thanks, Eric.)

But *Odelay*, together with the two Beck albums that followed—*Mutations* and, even more so, *Midnite Vultures*—had a longer-term and deeper effect on my writing in my first two novels than any of these works except for the Malamud (a big influence on *Ring On Deli*).

On *Odelay*, I cherished the humor, the potent fusion of many different kinds of American music, from blues to hip-hop, and the rich fabric of pop-culture allusion, just as I had a few years earlier with the landmark Beastie Boys album *Paul's Boutique* (like *Odelay*, it was produced by the Dust Brothers).

On *Mutations* and *Midnite Vultures*, I appreciated the soundscapes, which *Odelay* had pre-figured. To my ear they were analogous to what's sometimes going on in a novel. You're never really just reading the next word in a novel. You're reading it with the activated memory of what you've read already, including the sound of it, and with some anticipation, analogous to waiting for a resolving chord or the next beat, of what might come next.

Midnite Vultures was also playfully dirty. Who could forget the slamming-robot sex in the intro to "Get Real Paid" or the f-bomb that closes out "Mixed Bizness," a song in which Beck informs us that he is mixing business with a BDSM term that slant-rhymes with "pleasure." (The album owed a debt to Prince. One song, "Peaches and Cream," is more accurately described as a parody-tribute to Prince or even, simply, as a Prince song). An ounce of that randy humor infects my own work in select places, as close readers will note.

"Love and Theft"

The other album was Bob Dylan's *"Love and Theft"*. It came out while I was in the fall of my third year of law school. I had gotten more deeply into Dylan, especially that other later-career masterpiece *Time Out of Mind*, after returning from Orlando. At the same time, I had unwittingly stumbled on some earlier American music that I later learned had been the taproot of much of Dylan's work. At a used-CD store then on Church Street in Cambridge I bought a bunch of old folk and country-blues albums on the cheap. I'd first encountered this kind of music the summer that I was fourteen and, oversaturated with rap, picked up *Legends of the Blues: Volume 1*, a decent sampler, at a Strawberries tape store on Cape Cod. The Church Street stack was even more wide-ranging, and it led me to Harry Smith's *Anthology of American Folk Music*. I listened to that music endlessly as I waded my way through law school, taking consolation in the songs by playing them in my head through the long droning Socratic sessions. It'd be nice to think that those songs have influenced my writing too, though I couldn't say how.

I bought *"Love and Theft"* (the album title is in quotes, just as much of its contents could be) at about 9:02 a.m. on Tuesday, September 11, 2001, at the Tower Records in Harvard Square. A few minutes later, at a career-services office (I was exploring careers other than law) I saw on the office TV, around which everyone had gathered, that airplanes had smashed into the Twin Towers. Like nearly everyone else, I was diverted to listening to the news and, at one of those strangely close moments in American history—perhaps the last we'll ever have—to making sympathetic eye contact and instinctively chatting with strangers, who I met crossing Harvard Square or eating double cheeseburgers at Charlie's Kitchen.

When I finally settled down a week or two later with the CD of Dylan's latest, I was stunned. Here was another artist stealing—with love—from snippets and fragments of prior great songs and literature, including a yakuza's memoir but with loads of references to American folk music, history, culture, and fiction, all loves of mine (he channels Gatsby: of course you can repeat the past!). All while weaving this together with his own words into a distinct and whole new thing. Even better, it was energized by a kind of irrepressible will to live and to play.

I wanted to do that, to scour my loves, whether from history or culture (mostly but not all American) and fuse, blend, or mash them up into stories that worked and stood on their own, that came alive with their own kind of music. I hope that I pulled that off in some small, crazy way in my first two novels.

It's also possible those albums have not influenced my novels as much as I think they did, or that other albums I can't think of influenced them more. What I do know is that I was young then, with the wildest of dreams, and that life was so vivid that I absorbed my music—Dylan and Beck at the top of the list—well and deeply. I'll never forget it.

Acknowledgments

I'm going to keep this short because this book is. Deep gratitude to early readers Dan Visel (who also designed the book), Mark Travassos, Andrew Palid, David Zukowski, Frank Giroux, Rose Giroux, Joshua Greene, and Lawrence Pisto. Special thanks to Jasmine Chen for helping to clean up my cover image. All my love to family and friends.

ATTENTION ALL SHOPPERS!

Enjoy *Clare's Boutique*?
Scoop up *Ring On Deli*—Eric Giroux's
acclaimed debut novel about
Supermarkets and Democracy

When the Bounty Bag supermarkets erupt with
worker protests, deli-clerk Ray is forced to take a side.

WINNER, *National Indie Excellence Award*
WINNER, *Readers' Favorite Award*

"Quirky characters take a stand against a
supermarket in Giroux's nimble debut.... This
author has talent to burn."

—*Publishers Weekly*

"Giroux's prose is reminiscent of Richard Russo's
writing: intricate and incisive, though always
full of warmth and humor.... A well-balanced
comic tale that deftly grapples with larger
contemporary themes."

—*Kirkus*

"It has the charm of some heady contemporary
fable, in which the whole business model we call
America is turned back into a weirdly plausible,
almost utopian experiment."

—Robert Cohen, author of *Going to the Tigers:
Essays and Exhortations* and *Amateur Barbarians*

**Available wherever books are sold and at
newsalembooks.com. Ring on!**

WELCOME BACK TO PENNACOOK!

Eric Giroux returns to the
hard-luck hamlet of Pennacook, Massachusetts,
for *Zodiac Pets*: a comic novel about
Small Towns and Democracy!

Misfit Wendy Zhou confronts dark forces aiming to buy
her hometown and plunk a giant dome over it.

WINNER, *NYC Big Book Award*
FINALIST, *Foreword INDIES Award*
FINALIST, *National Indie Excellence Award*
DISTINGUISHED FAVORITE,
Independent Press Award

"A potent novel of growing up and facing the
world. … Giroux weaves a gripping narrative,
laced with humor, that interrogates and
encourages reflection on individuals' susceptibility
to the influence of those in power."
—*BookLife*

"Giroux keenly portrays a young girl's growing
awareness of the corruption and hubris of adults.
This comic novel has surprising depth."
—*Publishers Weekly*

"Zany, manic, absolutely crackers, *Zodiac Pets* is a
smart, snarky satire of American idealism crashing
headfirst into its mortal enemy: human nature."
—Stewart O'Nan, author of
The Speed Queen and *Last Night at the Lobster*

**Available wherever books are sold and at
newsalembooks.com.**